Nikki Maloney

Copyright © 2016 by Nikki Maloney

All rights reserved. This book or any portion thereof may not be reproduced or used in any manner whatsoever without the express written permission of the publisher except in the case of brief quotations in a book review.

Printed in the United States

ISBN-13: 978-1517725570
ISBN-10: 1517725577
LCCN: 2016903243
CreateSpace Independent Publishing Platform, North Charleston, SC

First Printing, February 2016

Pebble Beach®, The Lodge at Pebble Beach™, The Lone Cypress™, its image and The Heritage Logo are trademarks service marks and trade dress of Pebble Beach Company. Puppy Menu is copyright Pebble Beach Company. Used by permission.

For information contact :
www.NikkiMaloney.com

Please visit Amazon.com or NikkiMaloney.com for more titles in this series :

The Peppermints
BIG SUR

story by
Nikki Maloney

illustrated by
Christian Ridder

"Until one has loved an animal,
a part of one's soul remains
unawakened."

-Anatole France

To Goodie, for the gift of the
Peppermints and to his father Frank,
the original storyteller,
who always told the *truth*.

CONTENTS

CHAPTER ONE

Mr. and Mrs. Peppermint were enjoying a cool, late summer evening out on their screened-in porch. They talked over the rhythmic hum of the cicadas.

The male cicadas song made Mrs. Peppermint smile, as it reminded her of her youngest sister, Katy.

Mrs. Peppermint said, "When I was little I used to tease Katy and say that the cicadas were arguing over something she did. If you listen closely it sounds like they are saying, 'Katy did. Katy didn't. Katy did. Katy didn't.' "

Mr. Peppermint laughed, and winked lovingly at his wife.

Mr. Peppermint commented, "What a summer it has been. I just can't believe how the children have grown."

"What a long way Pete has come from a shy, diffident boy to a self-assured young man," Mrs. Peppermint added. "He is cutting almost every lawn on the cul-de-sac, and the neighbors report that he is doing an excellent job."

Mr. Peppermint continued, "Our sweet Patty has developed into a mature, independent, and beautiful young lady. She is a natural with animals and has established her own neighborhood pet sitting business."

"And our precocious, puckish Peggy has evolved and is now a cooperative, entertaining young Miss. She is quite helpful around the house, loves to bake, and boy does she have a witty sense of humor," said Mrs. Peppermint.

Mr. Peppermint said, "Oh and Philpot, our Potty, has certainly come into his own. He is showing a bona fide interest in music. He was sweeping the garage the other day and on the way back into the house he picked up the broom and strummed it giving his best Elvis impersonation.

"I have been thinking. I believe the kids are mature enough to handle the responsibility of getting a dog."

"Oh honey. That's a smashing idea. It would mean so much to them."

That night, Mr. and Mrs. Peppermint busied themselves upstairs packing for their trip. Mr. Peppermint had won *salesman of the year* and an all-expense paid vacation to California. Mr. Peppermint's mother, Mimi, was coming to stay with the children.

CHAPTER TWO

The next day, Mr. and Mrs. Peppermint hugged and kissed the children goodbye.

Then they drove to the airport and hopped on an afternoon flight. Arriving at San Francisco International Airport after their five-hour plane ride, they rented a car and set out for their three-hour drive along U.S. Highway 1 down to Pebble Beach.

Mrs. Peppermint was busy enjoying the view out her window. She marveled at the scenic views as they passed Half Moon Bay, Santa Cruz and Monterey. Soon, they arrived at the *Del Monte Lodge* at Pebble Beach.

They checked into their room right before sunset. Tired from their day of travel, they decided to order room service and pile up some *z*'s so they would be rested for their trip down to Big Sur the following day.

CHAPTER THREE

After sleeping in, Mr. and Mrs. Peppermint awoke the next morning, had breakfast, hopped in their car and began their journey down Big Sur Drive. The ride was quite curvy, and Mr. Peppermint became concerned when the rickety rental car wasn't responding to his driving.

It seemed like when he steered left, the car would go right, and when he steered right, the car would go left. This made for a precarious ride along the narrow, sinuous road beside the sheer cliffs. As they drove along the Bixby Creek Bridge, Mrs. Peppermint looked down in awe at the water below, and her blood pressure seemed to go up with every turn.

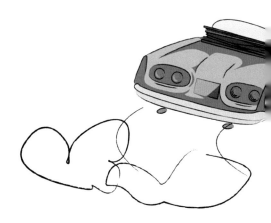

CHAPTER FOUR

Thankfully, after an exciting morning of travel, the Peppermints arrived in Big Sur at the *Nepenthe* restaurant. They had a lovely meal and enjoyed some sensational California wine.

After lunch, they decided to stretch their legs. Suddenly, Mrs. Peppermint heard a curious sound. She followed it and came upon a litter of puppies along the side of the restaurant. There was a sign that read, *Puppies 5 cents.*

She started to say, "Oh sweetheart, do you think…" while Mr. Peppermint asked, "Should we?"

They walked closer, entered the pen, and observed six, fluffy, black, Labrador puppies. They were all about the same size, but among them was one pocket-sized pup.

Mrs. Peppermint crouched down; the little fuzz ball came over and worked his way between her legs and looked up at her with big, sad eyes. Then he whimpered and grabbed hold of Mrs. Peppermint's slacks with his teeth and tugged back and forth as if saying, "Please don't leave without me!"

Mr. Peppermint said, "This dog loves you honey." He thought for a minute then asked, "Wouldn't it be a great surprise if we brought him home?"

Mrs. Peppermint shone with excitement. Mr. Peppermint scooped up the tiny creature with one hand and headed toward the cashier. He fished in his pocket for change, and pulled out a nickel.

At that point the puppy's owner said, "Don't bother, you can have him for free, seeing as though he's the runt of the litter and all."

Mr. and Mrs. Peppermint spent the entire afternoon at *Nepenthe* sitting on the outdoor terrace. Perched eight hundred feet above the immense redwood forest, they admired the cerulean Pacific Ocean and enjoyed the view of the Santa Lucia Mountains.

Big Sur

CHAPTER FIVE

When it was time to go, Mr. and Mrs. Peppermint climbed into their car. Mrs. Peppermint placed the puppy on her lap in the passenger seat, while Mr. Peppermint drove back to the *Del Monte Lodge* at Pebble Beach where they would spend the rest of their vacation. After a few minutes, the puppy became restless. Sniffing and whining like crazy, the animal strained to look out the window down toward the ocean.

Mr. Peppermint said, "Look honey, I think he wants to go down to the beach for a run."

Mrs. Peppermint looked out the window down to a splendid stretch of coastline. They pulled the car along the side of the road and carried the pup down a steep path onto sandy Pfeiffer Beach.

Mrs. Peppermint stood on the sand gazing at the water streaming through the portal rock. Mr. Peppermint set the puppy down, and the little guy wobbled toward the water. Just as he got to the edge, a wave broke right through the hole in the gigantic rock and onto the shore. It gave him such a fright that he stumbled into a back flip and lay exasperated on the sand.

CHAPTER SIX

Mr. Peppermint looked down at the pitiful pup and exclaimed, "He's such a tiny ball of fur; I wonder if he'll ever grow and be a big dog someday?"

Mrs. Peppermint admitted, "Oh, I don't think so but I just thought of a great name. *Big Sur.* We'll call him *Big Sur* even if he doesn't grow up to be big and strong, and it will always remind us of this incredible trip."

"What a great idea," said Mr. Peppermint.

They looked over at Big Sur and found him curled up on the sand fast asleep. Mrs. Peppermint lifted him up and cuddled him in her arms. They hiked back up the hill, slid into their car, and continued their ride up north.

It was dark when they arrived back at the *Lodge* and not until Mrs. Peppermint was about to enter did she contemplate whether or not pets were allowed.

Not knowing what to do, Mrs. Peppermint put Big Sur into her purse and walked right past the front desk and up to their room. Once inside, Big Sur woke with a start and immediately began whining. Mrs. Peppermint realized that they were fully unprepared for a dog. They had no food, no collar, and no leash. They would just have to improvise. Mr. Peppermint called room service.

The kitchen answered, "Room service, how may I help you?"

Mr. Peppermint thought quickly, "I'll have a hamburger."

"Yes sir, and how would you like that cooked?" replied the man.

After a slight pause, Mr. Peppermint answered, "Raw please."

The man hesitated then said, "Yes sir," and thought, "I can't wait to tell the boys in the kitchen."

Time went by and just as Mr. and Mrs. Peppermint were all cozy sitting by the fire in their pajamas, there came a knock on the door, "Room Service."

Quickly, Mrs. Peppermint put Big Sur out on the balcony, closed the sliding door, and drew the curtains.

The waiter came in, rolling the service cart in front of him. He came to a stop, paused, and

lifted the silver dome revealing the giant mound of raw meat on a plate.

Mr. Peppermint examined the plate, said, "Looks delicious, thank you Sir," and handed the waiter a tip. The waiter left the room awfully confused.

When the coast was clear, Mrs. Peppermint opened the door to the balcony, and Big Sur bounded into the room. Mr. Peppermint took the plate off the table and set it down in front of the hungry pup.

Big Sur swam in the surf, ran around, slept through the long car ride back to the *Lodge,* and here in front of him was a hamburger as big as he was. He slurped it down as best he could, pausing momentarily to look at Mr. and Mrs. Peppermint thinking, "I certainly picked the right people!"

When he ate all that he could, he waddled and tried to sit down, but his round tummy was so full that he just rolled over.

CHAPTER SEVEN

The next morning, Mr. Peppermint awoke for an early tee time. While he played a round of golf, Mrs. Peppermint attempted to take Big Sur down to the beach in her beach bag. It was early enough in the morning that she made it to the ocean without anyone noticing her secret.

Once again Big Sur would run all the way up toward the ocean, only to run away when the waves crashed on the beach.

Upon her return to the *Lodge*, Mrs. Peppermint noticed the most peculiar sight. There were dozens of dogs sitting on the outdoor patio having breakfast with their owners.

To her left, she spotted a statuesque blonde-haired woman sipping orange juice while her white Labrador ate a ground beef patty. A waitress refilled the black Labrador's water bowl, and the dogs' owner thanked the waitress and commented, "Finley's beef is cooked to perfection and thank you for refilling Max's water bowl."

To the right there was a white, toy poodle snacking on crunchy carrot sticks and a pair of Chihuahuas slurping up a savory dish of scrambled eggs and bacon.

Mrs. Peppermint approached the owner and asked, "Are you all staying here at the *Del Monte*?"

The woman replied, "Why honey, Louis, Minnie, and Poncho wouldn't stay anywhere else! In fact, they are continuing a tradition. The *Lodge* was our beloved Chico's favorite place to stay when he was still with us."

Mrs. Peppermint laughed when she realized the *Del Monte* was indeed pet-friendly, and there was no need for her to conceal her new fur baby.

Then, she focused her attention on two outstanding canines. The larger of the two had auburn hair with eyes the same shade as his fur, and he looked like a big teddy bear. The smaller one looked as if someone had painted the topside of him with black paint and the entire underside with white. He had impressive upright ears and tilted his head left and right observing everything around him.

Both dogs' fluffy tails wagged nonstop and increased in momentum as Mrs. Peppermint came closer.

Mrs. Peppermint remarked, "What gorgeous dogs you have!"

The dog's owner smiled and commented while pointing at the brown and then the black and white dog, "This is my dear Bear and his younger brother, Grizzly." Then Bear let out a loud bark saying hello.

Continuing on and entering the building, Mrs. Peppermint noticed a large, grey creature sitting beside a stunning woman who had the most sublime, black hair with waves like the ocean. Mrs. Peppermint failed to identify the species until she got close enough to ask the owner what it was.

The woman declared, "Oh my dear, I saw your confused face. Let me tell you that this is my Great Dane, Mojo. My other two darlings, Boss and Miss Roxanne are taking a nap up in the room."

Mrs. Peppermint observed the animal before her eyes and noted he was the size of a small horse, and she watched as he delicately dined on a breakfast of steak tartare.

CHAPTER EIGHT

Later in the day, Mr. Peppermint joined Mrs. Peppermint at the pool. He gasped when he saw Big Sur sleeping in the shade of the umbrella.

Quickly he threw a towel over the puppy to hide him. Mrs. Peppermint giggled and explained that pets were indeed welcome, and Mr. Peppermint let out a sigh of relief.

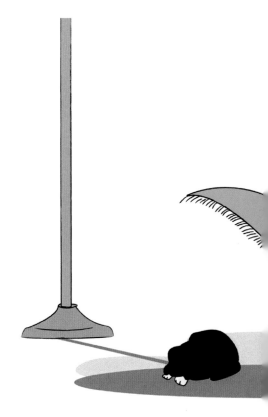

That night, Mr. and Mrs. Peppermint had a love-ly dinner while Big Sur had the special: **Char-Grilled Breast of Chicken with Peanut Butter Glaze**. He licked his chops and looked at the Peppermints as if to say, "This is the life!"

CHAPTER NINE

After a wonderful vacation, the next night, Mr. and Mrs. Peppermint flew home. Arriving at two o'clock in the morning, they walked softly into the house to find Potty, Peggy, Patty and Pete wide-awake sitting on the steps.

"I put them to bed hours ago, but they woke up and insisted they wait up for you," Mimi offered.

The children rubbed the sleep out of their eyes and said, "You're home! How was your trip?"

Mrs. Peppermint had Big Sur hidden in her trench coat. She slowly unwrapped the coat and whisper-yelled, "Surprise" as she revealed the sleepy creature.

"Oh, Mommy," Patty exclaimed. "A puppy? Is that our puppy? What's his name?"

"Yes and his name is Big Sur!" answered Mrs. Peppermint.

Big Sur opened his mouth wide in a yawn. The children marveled at their new family member and laughed at the teeny, tiny puppy.

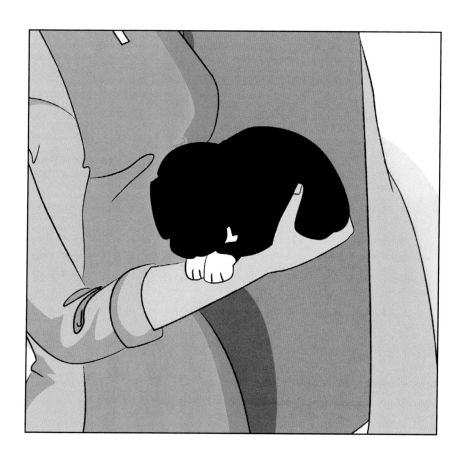

CHAPTER TEN

A few years went by and Pete was attending high school at the Prep. Patty, Peggy and Potty would walk down the hill to their school each day, and Big Sur would always follow them. At the bottom of the hill, they took the right turn onto Westbrook Place where Old Man Mr. Hunt and his little terrier, Blackie, greeted them. Blackie would look up; Big Sur would look down, and Blackie would give Sur a big slurp.

Big Sur would follow the children all the way to the end of the road, turn around, and make the return trip home up the hill on his own. Big Sur was so loyal that he would wait all day until the children came home.

After school, it was time for Sur to accompany Potty on his paper route where he would help Potty deliver the papers on the cul-de-sac. Some nights it would be so dark that Potty would have to use a flashlight, but he always felt safe with his good buddy Sur. On Friday nights Potty would collect the cash his neighbors owed him. Sometimes Mr. Smith had no money, and Big Sur would growl at him. Mr. Smith would then say, "Oh wait," and come back with the money to pay the bill. Potty and Big Sur made a great team.

On Saturday mornings, Potty would ride his bike all the way to the candy store to buy his favorite confections with the tips he had earned. He always saved enough money to buy Big Sur a bone from the butcher.

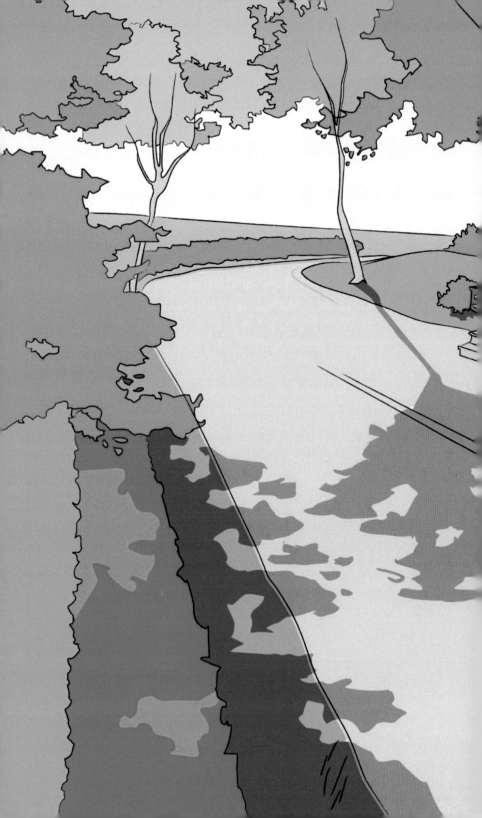

CHAPTER ELEVEN

One evening, Mr. and Mrs. Peppermint had a big party. Mrs. Peppermint cooked a beautiful steak filet and was letting it rest on the cutting board in the kitchen. Time went by, and Mr. Peppermint suggested, "I think our friends are getting hungry."

Mrs. Peppermint said, "I think you're right. Why don't you go in and slice the meat."

Mr. Peppermint went into the kitchen with Mrs. Peppermint close behind. They looked on the counter but did not see anything.

"Are you sure you took it out of the oven?" asked Mr. Peppermint.

Mrs. Peppermint replied, "Of course, I--"

Just then she looked down and saw Big Sur, eyes guilty, tail between his legs. He rolled over sideways, just like he did when he was a pup, and fell over holding his tummy.

Mrs. Peppermint glanced over at Mr. Peppermint, and they enjoyed their shared memory of their little pup who had grown into a sizeable dog.

He was so big, that when he stood on his hind

legs, he could rest his forearms right on Mr. Peppermint's shoulders.

THE END

Read this story again!

There are 42 peppermint sticks hidden in the pages of the story. The shapes of the peppermint sticks should look like the shapes below.

For a helpful guide to find all the hidden peppermint sticks and to discover more titles, visit **NikkiMaloney.com**

The Lodge
PEBBLE BEACH

Puppy Menu

Available from 8:00 a.m. to 10:00 p.m. through Room Service.

STARTERS
Bowl of Baby Carrots
Chilled and crunchy

SPECIALTIES

Scrambled Eggs and Bacon
*Two fresh whole eggs scrambled, applewood-
smoked bacon bits, and whole wheat toast mixed
together and served at room temperature*

Ground Beef Patty
*8 oz. patty cooked to order with or without
American cheese, served at room temperature*

Steak Tartare
*8 oz. hand-chopped
raw beef tenderloin*

Char-Grilled Breast of Chicken with
Peanut Butter Glaze
*Chopped mini-chunks of breast of chicken,
served at room temperature, paw lickin' good*

DESSERTS
A good puppy deserves to get dessert when they lick their bowl clean!

Chef Hui's Puppy Cookies
*Prepared by our award-winning Pastry Chef John Hui,
these cookies will be a lasting memory for any puppy*

Tongue Lickin' Peanut Butter
A generous scoop of smooth peanut butter in a bowl ready for feeding

BEVERAGE
One liter bottle Acqua Panna water

TOYS AND TREATS
The Pebble Beach Market offers puppy toys and treats that would make any puppy happy.

PUPPY CONCIERGE
*The Lodge Concierge has information on locations of nearby veterinarians, puppy sitters and
puppy-friendly places on the Monterey Peninsula for family excursions.*

HOUSEKEEPING
The Lodge Housekeeping Department cleans the guest rooms between 8:30 a.m. and 4:30 p.m. daily.
Nightly turndown service is offered between 5:30 p.m. and 9:30 p.m. Please make sure that your puppy
is not in the room unsupervised during those times. To schedule a specific time for service, contact
Housekeeping. Puppies must be on a leash while walking within the Resort.

The Terrace Lounge welcomes your puppy on a leash to sit outside with you while you enjoy a wonderful
dining experience. Monterey County prohibits dogs, except for service animals, in our indoor dining areas.
Thank you for your understanding.

Rev 7/11

Nikki Maloney

**I want to express my heartfelt thanks
to the following people:**

To Mom and Dad, Fran, Chrissy and Tim, I am blessed
to be part of such an incredible family.

To Steve: for your friendship and love *no matter what.*

To Alec, Sean, and Tatum: my eternal source of inspiration.
Thank you for remembering the little details.

To my friends and family, your support and shared enthusiasm
keep me motivated throughout the writing process.

To the adult readers and young listeners, especially those at
Gladwyne Elementary and Wenonah Elementary,
for their excitement and honest opinions.

To Dr. Murphy, truly one of the most generous people
I have ever met. Your wisdom and encouragement have
given me something I can never repay.
I am forever grateful.

To the many teachers and students from whom
I have learned. You all inhabit a special place in my heart.

To Neal and Katie, for the valuable insight on the history of The
Lodge at Pebble Beach, formerly known as the Del Monte Lodge.

Lastly, to Christian Ridder, an outstanding artist and
extraordinary human being, for reimagining *The Peppermints* and
approaching things from an original perspective.

About the Author

Nikki Maloney has enjoyed writing since attending her first poetry workshop at Fairfield Woods Library in Connecticut. She currently works as a Reading Specialist, and lives in Pennsylvania with her husband, three children, two dogs and guinea pig. This is her fifth children's book.

About the Illustrator

Christian Ridder has been drawing and painting all his life. He only began painting seriously in high school. He currently studies architecture in Philadelphia and hopes to incorporate what he loves about the past into the art and architecture of the future. This is what gives the nostalgic setting of *The Peppermints* such an appeal to him.

Made in the USA
Middletown, DE
20 April 2023

29181536R00031